A Sunburst Book
Michael di Capua Books
Farrar, Straus and Giroux

·Yellow & Pink·

William Steig

To some recent arrivals: Jonas, Jonathan,
Nathaniel, Max, Paige, Will, Serena

Two small figures made of wood were lying out in the sun one day, on an old newspaper. One was short, fat, and painted pink; the other was straight, thin, and painted yellow. It was hot and quiet, and they were both wondering.

After a while, the yellow one sat up and focused his gimlet eyes on the pink one. "Do I know you?" he asked.

"I don't think so," Pink answered.

"Do you happen to know what we're doing here?" asked Yellow.
"No," said Pink. "I don't even remember getting here."

"Me neither," said Yellow, looking all around. There were chick-
ens busy pecking a little way off, and farther back in the field some

dreamy cows. "I can't help wondering," he went on, "how we got to be here. It all seems new and strange. Who are we?"

Pink looked Yellow over. He found Yellow's color, his well-chiseled head, his whole form, admirable. "Someone must have made us," he said.

"How could anyone make something like me, so intricate, so perfect?" Yellow asked. "Or, for that matter, like you. And wouldn't we know who made us, since we had to be there when we got made?"

"And why," Yellow added, "would he leave us like this—with no explanation. I say we're an accident, somehow or other we just happened."

Pink couldn't believe what he heard; he started laughing. "You mean these arms I can move this way and that, this head I can turn in any direction, this breathing nose, these walking feet, all of this just happened, by some kind of fluke? That's preposterous!"

"Don't laugh," said Yellow. "Just stop and reflect. With enough time, a thousand, a million, maybe two and a half million years, lots of unusual things could happen. Why not us?"

"Because it's impossible! It's absolutely out of the question! How could we just happen? Would you mind explaining?"

Yellow got up and began pacing. He kicked a pebble aside. "Well, it could be something like this, I'm not saying exactly. Suppose a

branch broke off a tree and fell on a sharp rock in just the right way, so that one end split open and made legs. So there you have legs."

"Then winter came and this piece of wood froze and the ice split the mouth open. There's your mouth. Then maybe one day a big hurricane took that piece of wood and sent it tumbling down a rocky

hill with little bushes, and it got bumped and chipped and brushed and shaped this way and that. Sand blowing in the wind might have helped with the smoothing."

"That piece of wood could have hung around at the bottom of that hill for eons, until one day—*Zing!*—lightning struck in such a way as to make arms, fingers, toes."

"All right," Pink interrupted, "what about eyes? What about ears, what about nostrils?"

Yellow sat down on a stone to do more thinking.

"Eyes," he said, "could have been made by insects boring in, or by woodpeckers, maybe even by hailstones of exactly the right size hitting repeatedly in just the right places."

"Hmm," said Pink. He clasped his hands behind him. "How come we can see out of these holes the woodpecker made? And hear?"

"Because that's what eyes and ears are for, dummy. What else would you do with them? Those cows over there see with their big eyes. This ant sees with his teeny eyes. We see with ours."

"Okay," said Pink. "Let's say you're right, just for the sake of conversation. Do you mean to tell me all those odd things happened

not only once but twice, so that there's two of us? The branch fell off the tree, it hit the rock, it rolled down the hill, lightning struck, the woodpecker pecked, etc., etc."

"Why not?" said Yellow. "In a million years—I didn't say five seconds—the same thing could easily happen twice over. A million years takes a very long time. Branches do break, winds are always

blowing, there's always some lightning, and some hail, and so forth and so on."

"But you and I are so different," said Pink. "How come?"

"That only proves what I'm saying!" cried Yellow. "It's all accidental! You're probably a different kind of wood. You must have rolled down a different kind of hill, a soft, mushy one perhaps."

Pink was not satisfied with these explanations. He suddenly gave Yellow a challenging look. "Explain this," he said. "How come we're painted the way we are?"

Yellow took a few circular turns pondering this question. "The paint," he muttered, "the paint. Well, suppose when we rolled down those hills, or whatever it was we rolled down, we rolled through some paint someone had spilled. Pink for you . . ."

"Yellow for me."

"And it came out so neat and symmetrical?" Pink said. "With perfect edges, in just the right places? And there were three drops of white paint in a straight line for my buttons, and three black drops for yours? What about that, my yellow friend?"

Yellow was silent. He leaned against a tree stump, scratching his wooden head. "I can't answer all the questions," he said finally. "Some things will have to remain a mystery. Maybe forever. But why are we arguing on such a fine day?"

Just then a man who needed a haircut came shambling along, humming out of tune.

He picked up Pink and looked him over. Then he picked up Yellow and looked him over. "Nice and dry," he said.

He tucked them both under his arm and headed back where he'd come from.

"Who is this guy?" Yellow whispered in Pink's ear.

Pink didn't know.